For Lucy, who makes every Christmas the best one ever.

First published 2015 by Macmillan Children's Books
an imprint of Pan Macmillan,
20 New Wharf Road, London N1 9RR
Associated companies throughout the world
www.panmacmillan.com

ISBN: 978-1-5098-3665-9

Text and illustrations copyright © Ben Mantle 2015
Moral rights asserted.

1 3 5 7 9 8 6 4 2

A CIP catalogue record for this book is available from the British Library.

Printed in China

The Best Christmas Present Ever!

To: Bear
From: Squirrel

Ben Mantle

MACMILLAN CHILDREN'S BOOKS

Bear had a funny feeling he had forgotten something.

He'd already washed
behind his ears,

and shampooed and
styled his fur.

He just couldn't remember what it was. Maybe a walk would help.

Bear had just left his house when he bumped into his best friend Squirrel.

"FOUR SLEEPS TILL CHRISTMAS!" shouted
Squirrel excitedly. "I've got you such a great gift, Bear.
I can't wait to give it to you!"

To: Bear
From: Squirrel

Oh no! Bear had forgotten to get Squirrel a present.

"There must be something amazing in that big box," thought Bear.
"I'll have to think of an extra special present for Squirrel."

Bear looked at the cold snow. "That's it!" he thought.
"I'll knit Squirrel a Christmas jumper."

He knitted all day,
clickity-click,

and all night,
clickity-clack,
until the jumper
was finished.

There was just one *tiny* problem . . .

Bear was not very good at knitting.

"I can't give this to Squirrel," he moaned. "It's the *worst* Christmas present ever!"

Now there were only THREE SLEEPS till Christmas.
Bear was feeling worried.

"Owl will know what to give Squirrel," thought Bear.

"Why don't you paint Squirrel a picture?" suggested Owl when
Bear paid him a visit.
"What a brilliant idea!" said Bear. "I will paint him a portrait."

Bear rushed home and got to work.

He painted all day,
splash,

and all night, **splat,**
until the painting
was complete.

It was absolutely . . .

TERRIBLE!

Now there were only TWO SLEEPS till Christmas.
What was Bear going to do? Maybe Fox would know.

"It's nearly Christmas," Bear groaned to Fox later
that day.
"I know, exciting!" said Fox. "Have a slice of cake."
"But I don't know what to give Squirrel," Bear sighed.
He sat by the fire and thought . . .

"I know! I'll build him a rocking chair like this," Bear decided.

Bear rushed out and collected a big pile of wood.

He spent all day sawing, scritch-scratch,

and all night hammering,
tap-tap-BANG.

Then he added the finishing touch . . .

CRUNCH! What a calamity!

There was only ONE SLEEP left till Christmas and Bear still had nothing to give Squirrel.

He threw the pieces of chair onto the pile of ruined presents.

Suddenly Bear was struck by a fantastic idea.
Squirrel was going to love it!

There were no sleeps left.
Christmas had arrived!
Bear and Squirrel were having
a fabulous time drinking
hot chocolate and singing
their favourite songs.

But they couldn't wait any longer to open their presents.
"I'm going first!" said Bear, leading Squirrel outside.

"Ooh, what could it be?" said Squirrel as he pulled off the wrapping.

"A sledge!" he squealed. "This is the best Christmas present *ever!*"

"Thank you Bear," Squirrel shouted. "Jump on!"

But there wasn't quite enough room for two.

"Maybe I should get your present," mumbled Squirrel.

Squirrel ran off and came back with the box.
"Merry Christmas, Bear!" he smiled.
Bear untied the ribbon excitedly and looked inside.

"It's empty," said Bear.
"All the best boxes are empty,"
replied Squirrel. "Just imagine
the things we can do with it!"

"Come on Bear," shouted Squirrel.
"We're going to have so much fun!"

And he was absolutely right . . .

because now they BOTH had
the best Christmas presents ever.